ROMAN NUMERALS I to MM

NUMERABILIA ROMANA UNO AD DUO MILA

LIBER DE DIFFICILLIMO COMPUTANDO NUMERUM

Arthur Geisert

Houghton Mifflin Company Boston

For art teachers
Gerald Brommer, *age* LXIX
and
Reinhold Marxhausen, *age* LXXIV

Walter Lorraine (wn) Books

Copyright © 1996 by Arthur Geisert

All rights reserved. For information about permission to reproduce selections from this book, write to Permissions, Houghton Mifflin Company, 215 Park Avenue South, New York, New York 10003.

www.houghtonmifflinbooks.com

Library of Congress Cataloging-in-Publication Data

Geisert, Arthur.
    Roman numerals I to MM=Numerabilia romana uno ad duo mila / Arthur Geisert.
        p. cm.
    Summary: Introduces Roman numerals, and by counting pigs in the illustrations, the reader can reinforce the mathematical concept.
    CL ISBN 0-395-74519-5   PA ISBN 0-618-15321-7
    1. Roman numerals — Juvenile literature. 2. Counting — Juvenile literature. [1. Roman numerals. 2. Counting.] I. Title.
OA141.3.G45 1996
513.5'5'0148—dc20

95-36247
CIP
AC

Printed in the United States of America
WOZ 10 9 8 7 6

NUMERABILIA ROMANA UNO AD DUO MILA

LIBER DE DIFFICILLIMO COMPUTANDO NUMERUM

Seven letters stand for numbers called Roman numerals. Used alone or in various combinations, they will make every number. The letters are: I, V, X, L, C, D, and M.

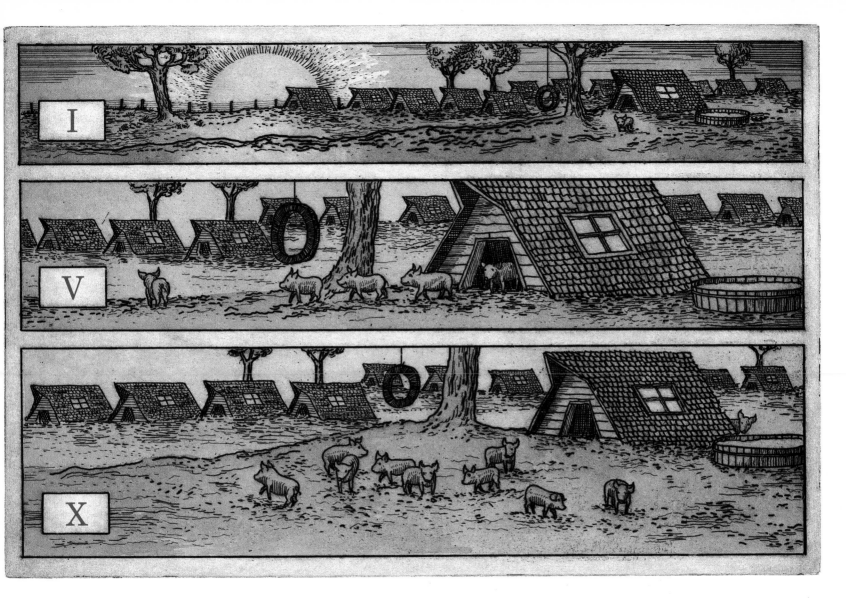

Count the number of pigs to find the value of each numeral.

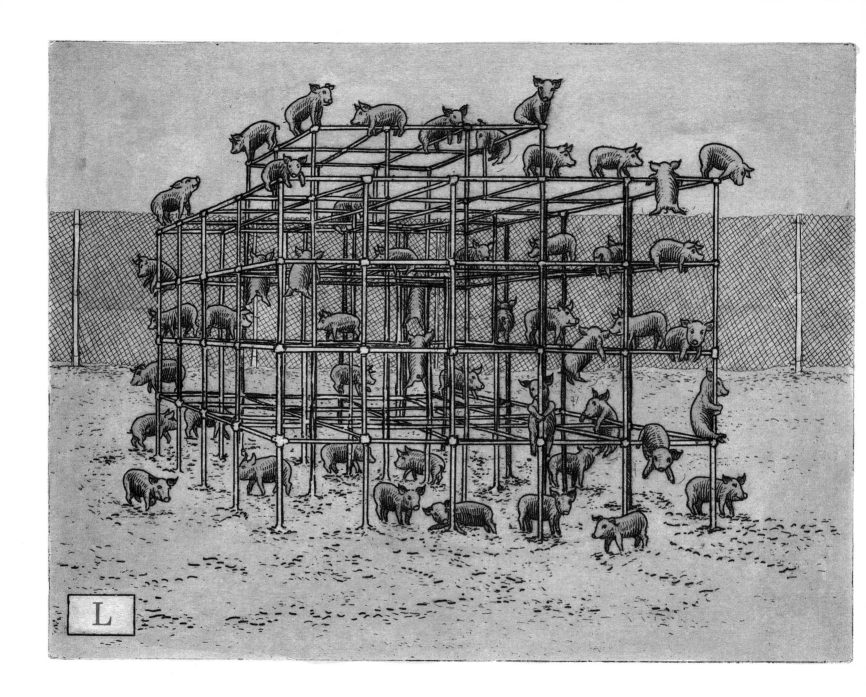

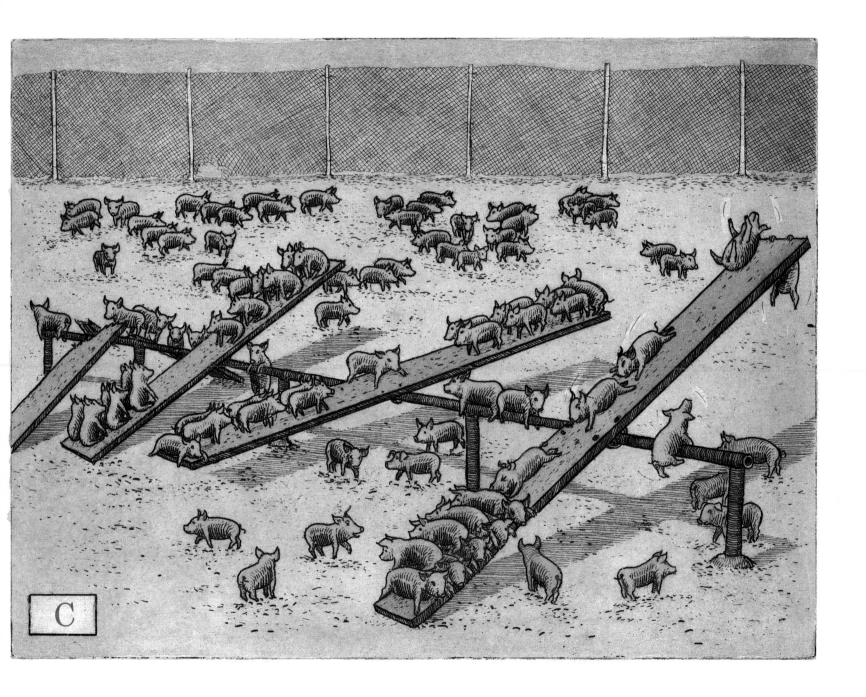

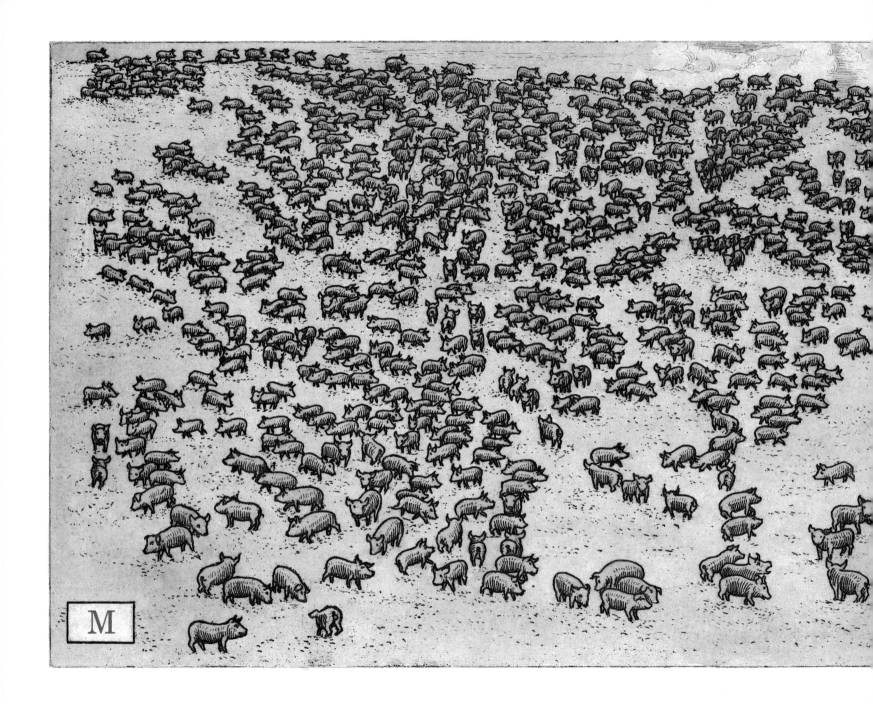

Roman numerals are written and read from left to right. If numerals of equal value are placed side by side, they are added.
I, X, and C may be used two and three times in a row.

V, L, and D are not used in a row because, when added, they total an existing numeral. VV=X, so X is used instead. Likewise, LL=C and DD=M.

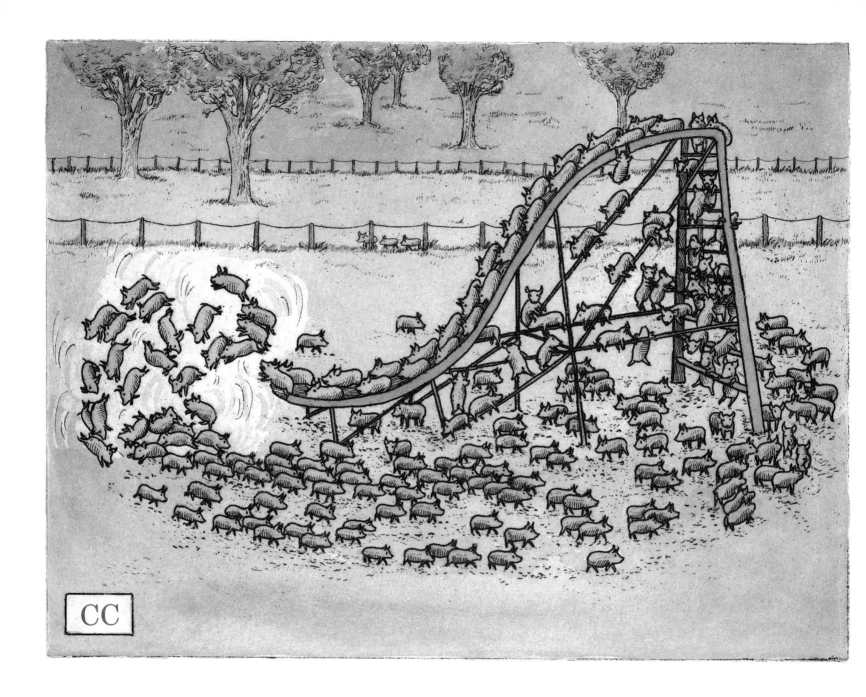

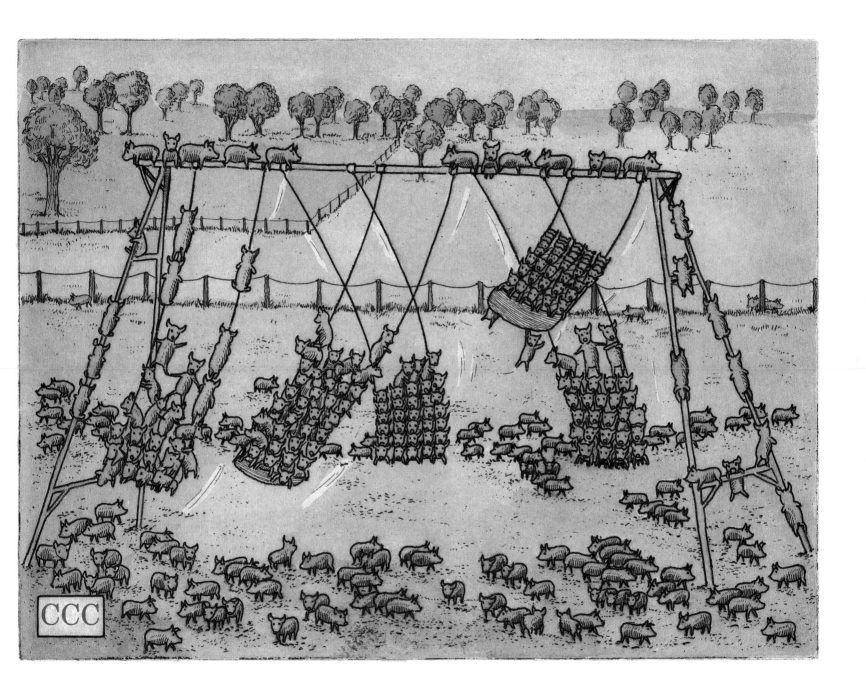

MM

M is the largest Roman numeral. It may also be used two and
three times in a row, as may I, X, and C. However, unlike I, X, and C,
M may be repeated many times.

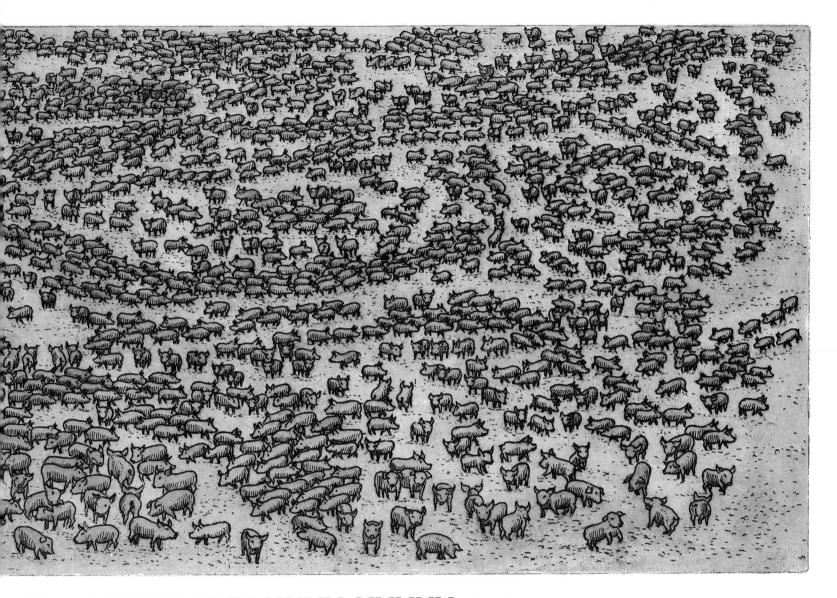

There is M, MM, MMM, MMMM, MMMMM, etcetera.

Numbers are made by adding and subtracting. When writing a Roman numeral, the largest numeral is written first, followed by numerals of equal or lesser value.

These numerals are added. However, when a smaller numeral appears before a larger numeral, it is subtracted from that numeral. IV and IX are examples.

Numerals that involve subtraction always have a four or nine
in that number. XIV and XIX are examples.

In a long number, subtraction may take place more than once.
This often happens in dates. MCMXC, nineteen ninety, is an example.

The best way to learn Roman numerals is to use them.
If you don't know what the numerals listed are,
count the objects in the picture to find out.

X   Pig Houses   V   Cows
III Tractors   XI   Evergreen trees
IV Water tanks   IX   Storage bins

II Tire swings VII Clouds
I Eighteen Twelve IV Birds
X Sandbags IV Hands

I Nineteen Twenty-two	II Eagles
IX Flowerpots	I Sixteen Twenty
XVI Gopher holes	XX Chain links

I   Eighteen Sixty-one   III   Trash cans

I   Nineteen Five   VL   Pigs

IV   Stone posts   I   Seventeen Fifty

XVIII	Bottles		I	Eighteen Ninety
I	Seventeen Sixty-six		LIV	Boiler bolts
IV	Brown jugs		XIII	Bricks

V	Saw blades	XXXVI	Pigs
I	Nineteen Hundred	I	Nineteen Forty-one
III	Urns	VI	Birds

This Book Contains

XII Stumps

XXXII Pages

VII Tire swings

III Weathervanes

XXVI Birds

I Bell

V Barrels

II Mice

IX Cannonballs

V Pig statues

II Sundials

VII Cows

MMMMDCCCLXIV Pigs